God Made You

Children's Catholic Book for Girls

Printed in the USA

God made you perfectly you;
Wonderfully made, divinely
assembled

I praise you. I am wonderfully made.

-Psalms 138:14

Your laugh, your smile, your hands and your toes

God knit you together, we watch you grow

You created me. You knit me together inside my mother's womb.

-Psalms 139:13

Oh, you, perfect you

The greatest of these is love
– 1 Corinthians 13:13

The way you run, the way
you huddle
Your beautiful joy, the way
you cuddle

Your heart has grown so very dear; Holding God's truth, it's all so clear

Love rejoices in the truth.
– 1 Corinthians 13:4-7

You are special, you are loved.
You are certainly our gift
from above.

We love because He first loved us.

-1 John 4:19

But most importantly, you are God's Daughter. Made in His image, He is your heavenly Father.

God created us in His own image.

– Genesis 1:27

He has plans, this you will see
Plans for you, plans for me

God knows the plans He has for you.
– Jeremiah 29:11

The plans for you are just for you

Wonderful things only you can do

All your hopes, all your dreams

God blesses you…

– Psalm 2:12

All you do, all you will be

Will shine God's love for all
to see

It is wonderful living in God's unity.
– Psalm 133:1

Just by being you, wonderful you

You are perfectly wonderful
to me!

A wise child brings joy to his parents.
– Proverbs 15:20

The Sign of the Cross

In the name of the Father, and of the Son, and of the Holy Spirit, Amen.

Hail Mary

Hail Mary full of Grace, the Lord is with thee. Blessed are thou among women and blessed is the fruit of thy womb Jesus. Holy Mary Mother of God, pray for us sinners now and at the hour of our death Amen.

Jesus, Mary and Joseph, Pray for Us

Our Father

Our Father, Who art in Heaven, hallowed be Thy name; Thy Kingdom come, Thy will be done on earth as it is in Heaven. Give us this day our daily bread; and forgive us our trespasses as we forgive those who trespass against us; and lead us not into temptation, but deliver us from evil. Amen.

Glory Be

Glory be to the Father and to the Son and to the Holy Spirit. As it was in the beginning is now, and ever shall be, world without end. Amen.